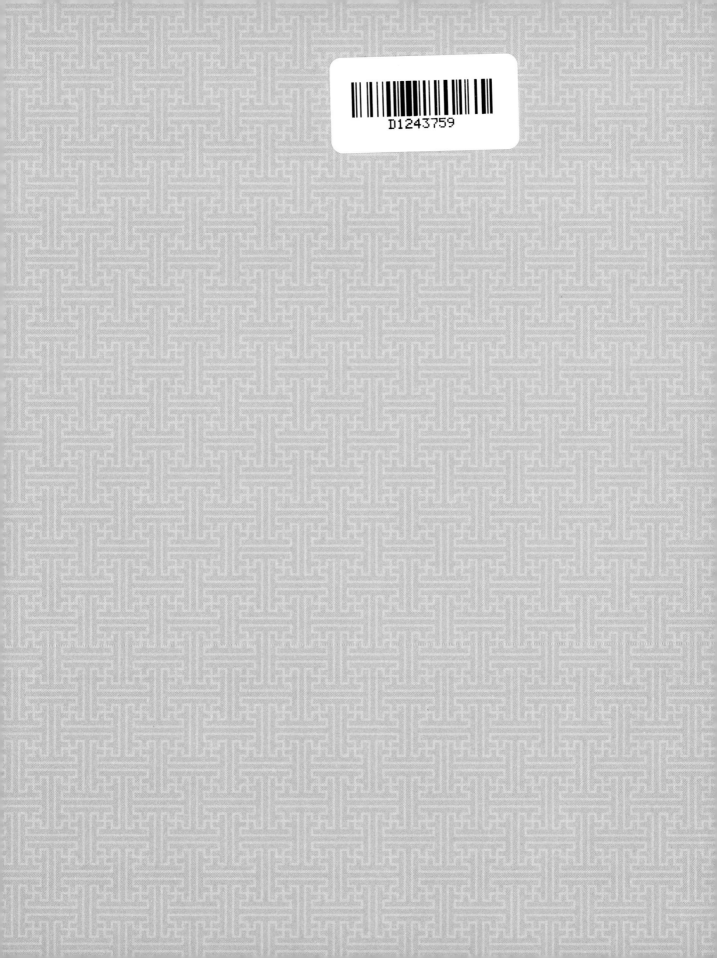

CATKWONDO

by Lisl H. Detlefsen   art by Erin Hunting

CAPSTONE EDITIONS
a capstone imprint

For my black belt boys and for the Park Institute team, especially Master John Chrystal — L.D.

To my lifetime muses Edith, Louie, Whiskers, and Matilda — E.H.

Catkwondo is published by
Capstone Editions, a Capstone imprint
1710 Roe Crest Drive
North Mankato, Minnesota 56003
www.capstonepub.com

Library of Congress Cataloging-in-Publication Data is available on the Library of Congress website.

ISBN: 978-1-68446-100-4 (hardcover)
ISBN: 978-1-68446-101-1 (eBook PDF)

Summary: As a new student of taekwondo, Kitten is eager to break a board, but Master Cat and her fellow students help her learn to focus, practice, and persevere.

Designer: Brann Garvey

Design elements: Shutterstock: kong mi jin (endsheets)

Special thanks to Dani Moran for sharing her expertise in taekwondo and Korean culture. The author would also like to thank Yangsook Choi, Jaekwan Yum, and Bohee Lim.

Printed and bound in China.
3322

TAEKWONDO OATH

- 🐾 I will observe the principles of taekwondo.

- 🐾 I will respect the instructor and all senior ranks.

- 🐾 I will never misuse taekwondo.

- 🐾 I will be a champion of freedom and justice.

- 🐾 I will build a more peaceful world.

Observe the master.

He is smart.

He is strong.

He wears his black belt with honor and dignity.

Observe the new student.

She is eager.

She is energetic.

She wears her white belt in a crumpled knot.

"Let's fix your dhee, Kitten jeja. Tying your belt properly takes practice," says Master Cat. "There, much better!"

"When can I break a board, sabeomnim?" Kitten asks.

"One step at a time. In taekwondo, you must prepare both body and mind. First you will learn your moves: stances, blocks, punches, and kicks. Then I'll teach you to combine these moves into a pattern. Watch me."

"See? Use those paws!"

Kitten is excited to give it a try.

Swoosh swoosh kick

PLOP!

"Keep trying, Kitten jeja. Cats should always land on their feet!"

"Yes, sabeomnim," says Kitten.

Swoosh swoosh kick

PLOP!

"I didn't hear your kihap," says Master Cat.

"Try again, on the count of three:

Hana, dul, set!"

KERPLUNK!

Kitten groans. "I'll never be ready to break a board."

"Slow down, Kitten jeja. Learning taekwondo takes time," Master Cat says. "Remember to keep your tail out of the way."

"Like this?"

Whoosh Whoosh Swish

"Much better, Kitten jeja!" says Master Cat.

"I'll see you next class."

At home Kitten practices her poomsae. She studies the goals of taekwondo.

In time she earns her yellow belt.

"Now can I break a board?" she asks.

"Not yet, Kitten jeja," says Master Cat. "First you must begin to spar and practice your kick for breaking."

Class by class and kick by kick, Kitten learns.

A blue belt helps her. "Time to warm up, Kitten!"

A red belt helps her.

"Get ready for sparring, Kitten!"

A black belt helps her.

"Let's see your form, Kitten!"

Master Cat helps with the hardest part of all.

"Try your breaking kick again, Kitten jeja."

After weeks and weeks of practice . . .

"Time for testing," says Master Cat. "Let's see what you've learned. Charyot! Joonbi! Shijak!"

"Go, Kitten!" the color belts cheer.

"C'mon, Kitten! Power through that board!" the black belts cheer.

"Concentrate, Kitten jeja. You can do it!" Master Cat cheers.

Kitten closes her eyes.

She takes a deep breath.

READY!
STEADY!

Observe the master.

He is pleased.

He is proud.

He holds a symbol of Kitten's hard work.

Observe the student.

She has strength.

She has skill.

She ties her new orange belt with joy.

Taekwondo means "art of foot and fist." It is a Korean martial art practiced all over the world. Here are a few of the Korean terms used in taekwondo that were included in the story.

---

dhee 띠 (dee)—belt

dobok 도복 (doe-boke)—a taekwondo uniform

dojang 도장 (doe-jahng)—a taekwondo school or training hall

charyot 차렷 (cha-r-yuh-t)—attention or attention stance

hana, dul, set 하나, 둘, 셋 (ha-nah, dool, set)—one, two, three

jeja 제자 (jay-jah)—student of taekwondo

joonbi 준비 (june-bee)—ready or ready stance

kihap 기합 (kee-hop)—the sound made when performing certain moves in taekwondo; usually a short, one-syllable sound such as "Uht!"

poomsae 품새 (poom-say)—a series of moves combined into a pattern; also called forms

sabeomnim 사범님 (sah-bum-nim)—a taekwondo instructor or master (of fifth-degree black belt level or higher)

shijak 시작 (she-jock)—begin